This is Tina!

Tina likes being with Mommy more than anything.

Sometimes she plays with her toys and sometimes she helps Mommy.

While Mommy puts Tina's brother in his crib, Tina helps by bringing a giant stack of blankets from the laundry.

Mommy says, "I have something to show you while Geordie takes his nap. Something wonderful."

4

Then Mommy brings a giant stack of boxes from the garage.

What can it be?

SANTA STUFF

5

Look - it's Christmas in there! Shiny glass balls. Ribbons and fancy paper. Decorations for a tree. The tiny painted birds Uncle Claude sent from Japan and the beaded star from India.

And here's the wreath Grandma
made with pinecones from her yard.

Each treasure has a story and Tina loves stories.

Sometimes Tina pretends she is the curious monkey or the hungry bear. Sometimes she is a giant or the captain of a big sailing ship.

Tina likes to imagine herself in all kinds of stories.

Oh, boy – it's the Santa doll! Mommy fluffs the white fur on Santa's coat and wipes his shiny black boots. Tina says, "He has such a happy face, Mommy. Tell me about Santa."

"I love the Santa story," says Mommy. "It's all about giving. That must be what makes Santa so happy. And at Christmastime, with so many people giving gifts to each other, it's like a great big Santa game with lots of different ways to play."

Sometimes it's about elves making toys or a reindeer shining his bright nose through a foggy night. And there are chimneys and stockings and a sack full of presents and "What do you want?" and "Ho-Ho-Ho!" and always, always, always surprise gifts from Santa. Any time someone starts talking about Santa, we get to play too.

*T*ina wants to play now. "Can I be an elf and make toys?" she asks.

"Oh, yes!" says Mommy. "Elves must be very clever to make so many kinds of toys, don't you think?"

13

Just then the doorbell rings. It's Mr. Amano from down the street. When Mr. Amano sees Tina he says, "Hey, Tina. What do you want Santa to bring you for Christmas?"

Tina looks at Mommy and her eyes get really big. It's time to play the Santa game with Mr. Amano.

$\mathcal{T}$ina runs to Mr. Amano and leans close to his ear and whispers, "I want magic tools for making toys just like the elves."

Then she giggles and waves and runs to her room to play elves with her dolls, "Bye, Mr. Amano."

The next day Tina is playing at Jeh's house. Jeh says that Santa brings a big fancy tree to his family on Christmas Eve. But Jeh is worried how Santa will get inside since they don't have a chimney.

Then Jeh gets an idea, "What if the reindeer land Santa's sleigh in the back yard? Then Santa can come in the kitchen door."

J eh runs to ask his dad, "Can we please leave the door unlocked for Santa?"

Jeh's dad laughs, "I think Santa will just have to use his magic key." Then he winks at Jeh and Tina.

"Yes!" shouts Jeh, jumping up and down. Jeh likes magic.

At the park, Tina hears the big kids talk about writing letters to Santa.

If Mommy helps her with the writing, Tina has some ideas for her own letter.

18

That night, Mommy has an idea too. She gives Tina three cards - all just alike. She reads the words to Tina: "FROM SANTA." Then Mommy tells Tina her big Santa idea.

Dear Santa,
Did you ever have a nickname when you were a kid? Please write me back.
(Little) Andy

Dear Santa,
How is Mrs Claus? I think she mite like to ride. My mom is relly good with directns and Mu

Tina's friend, Mrs. Elkins, lives next door. She walks very slowly and worries about falling down.

Mommy says that in the morning Tina can surprise Mrs. Elkins. She can get her newspaper from the sidewalk and put it near her front door. Tina can leave one of her FROM SANTA cards with the newspaper for Mrs. Elkins to find.

Mommy whispers, "It will be our secret."

"But I thought Santa gives toys to children," says Tina.

"Oh, he does," says Mommy. "But Santa's so sneaky and so full of surprises, I like to think he has fun giving to everyone. And there are different ways of giving, you know. Lots of gifts come wrapped in fancy paper, but an **act of kindness** can be a gift too. You'll see."

First thing the next morning – even before breakfast –
Mommy pulls Tina's coat right over her pajamas.

"Quick, Tina. Quick! Hurry, hurry!"

𝓜ommy watches as Tina rushes outside to get the newspaper and take it to Mrs. Elkins' door.

Tina puts the FROM SANTA card right on top and runs back to Mommy.

23

At home, Tina and Mommy look out the window.

They wait and watch.

And watch and wait.

And then – it happens.

The door opens and Mrs. Elkins slowly steps out.

Look − there is the newspaper right at her feet!

She picks it up and sees the card Tina put on top.

Mrs. Elkins studies the card.

Then she looks up the street
– and down the street.

Mrs. Elkins smiles - and presses the card to her heart.

Mrs. Elkins is happy!

"Oh, Mommy! That was so much fun. Mrs. Elkins doesn't even know it was from me!"

"And I still have more cards. What can I do with them?"
asks Tina.

Mommy pulls Tina close and kisses her,
"You're so full of sweet ideas and happy surprises.
You'll think of something wonderful all by yourself."

29

A ND SO CAN YOU!

www.TheSantaStory.com

Print **FROM SANTA** cards (unlimited & free) for all your giving!

Download the song *I'm Being Santa* for free!

See the *I'm Being Santa* music video!

Get your free audio version of this book as read by the author!
at www.TheSantaStory.com/Tina